This book belongs to _____

It was given
to me by _____

THE HAIL MARY

written and illustrated by
Joan Hutson

St. Paul Books & Media

Library of Congress Cataloging-in-Publication Data

Hutson, Joan.
    Hail Mary / written and illustrated by Joan Hutson.
        p.   cm.
    Summary: A presentation of the prayer known as the Hail Mary.
    ISBN 0-8198-3324-X
    1. Ave Maria—Juvenile literature.   [1. Hail Mary.] I. Title.
BX2175.A8H82 1987   87-19399
242' .74—do19   CIP
                                                                                  AC

Printed in the U.S.A., by the Daughters of St. Paul
50 St. Paul's Ave., Boston, MA 02130

St. Paul Books & Media is the publishing house of the Daughters of St. Paul,
an international congregation of women religious serving the Church with the
communications media.

         2 3 4 5 6 7 8 9   99 98 97 96 95 94 93 92

THE HAIL MARY

Hail Mary full of grace, Hail Mary full of grace, Hail Mary full of grace, Ha

Hail Mary, full of grace

the Lord is with thee

blessed art thou among women

and blessed is the fruit of thy womb, Jesus.

Holy Mary, Mother of God

pray for us sinners, now and at the hour of our death.

AMEN.

Joan Hutson is a woman of many talents. The mother of seven, she is also an author, artist, educator and musician.

Her books include: *The Wind Has Many Faces* (Abbey Press), *Heal My Heart, O Lord* (Ave Maria Press), *An Instrument of Your Peace* (Doubleday), *Hunger for Wholeness* (Ave Maria Press), *I Think I Know* (Ave Maria Press), *The Lord's Prayer* (Standard Publishing), *Love Never Ever Ends* (Standard Publishing), *Creation, Praise* (Harold Shaw Publishers), *Heaven and Earth* (Concordia Publishing House), *It's Important* (St. Paul Books & Media) *My Happy Ones* (St. Paul Books & Media), *The Legend of the Nine Talents* (St. Paul Books & Media). She has also published approximately fifteen magazine articles.

She has illustrated many books, including most of her own, and there is a continuing exhibit of her paintings at Tri-County Hospital, in her hometown of Wadena, Minnesota.

As an educator, Mrs. Hutson has taught elementary school, high-school religion, and art and music classes for adults.

She is a liturgical guitarist and has been organist and choir director for her parish.

Bringing the message of God's love to His little ones is one of her specialties.

St. Paul Book & Media Centers

ALASKA
  750 West 5th Ave., Anchorage, AK 99501 907-272-8183.
CALIFORNIA
  3908 Sepulveda Blvd., Culver City, CA 90230 310-397-8676.
  1570 Fifth Ave. (at Cedar Street), San Diego, CA 92101 619-232-1442
  46 Geary Street, San Francisco, CA 94108 415-781-5180.
FLORIDA
  145 S.W. 107th Ave., Miami, FL 33174 305-559-6715; 305-559-6716.
HAWAII
  1143 Bishop Street, Honolulu, HI 96813 808-521-2731.
ILLINOIS
  172 North Michigan Ave., Chicago, IL 60601 312-346-4228; 312-346-3240.
LOUISIANA
  4403 Veterans Memorial Blvd., Metairie, LA 70006 504-887-7631; 504-887-0113.
MASSACHUSETTS
  50 St. Paul's Ave., Jamaica Plain, Boston, MA 02130 617-522-8911.
  Rte. 1, 885 Providence Hwy., Dedham, MA 02026 617-326-5385.
MISSOURI
  9804 Watson Rd., St. Louis, MO 63126 314-965-3512; 314-965-3571.
NEW JERSEY
  561 U.S. Route 1, Wick Plaza, Edison, NJ 08817 908-572-1200.
NEW YORK
  150 East 52nd Street, New York, NY 10022 212-754-1110.
  78 Fort Place, Staten Island, NY 10301 718-447-5071; 718-447-5086.
OHIO
  2105 Ontario Street (at Prospect Ave.), Cleveland, OH 44115 216-621-9427.
PENNSYLVANIA
  214 W. DeKalb Pike, King of Prussia, PA 19406 215-337-1882; 215-337-2077.
SOUTH CAROLINA
  243 King Street, Charleston, SC 29401 803-577-0175.
TEXAS
  114 Main Plaza, San Antonio, TX 78205 512-224-8101.
VIRGINIA
  1025 King Street, Alexandria, VA 22314 703-549-3806.
CANADA
  3022 Dufferin Street, Toronto, Ontario, Canada M6B 3T5 416-781-9131.